Hugh Goldie

Memoir of King Ëyo VII of Old Calabar

A Christian King of Africa

Hugh Goldie

Memoir of King Ëyo VII of Old Calabar
A Christian King of Africa

ISBN/EAN: 9783744762571

Printed in Europe, USA, Canada, Australia, Japan

Cover: Foto ©Raphael Reischuk / pixelio.de

More available books at **www.hansebooks.com**

KING ËYO VII.

OF OLD CALABAR,

A CHRISTIAN KING

IN AFRICA.

Old Calabar
UNITED PRESBYTERIAN MISSION PRESS
1894.

At the suggestion of Mr. John Bishop, a much esteemed fellow-labourer in the mission, I drew up this memoir of our departed friend, King Èyö. At Mr. Bishop's desire the M. S. was put into his hand, his intention being to produce it as a specimen of the work of the Mission Press. He had just commenced putting it in type when a disease laid hold on him, which issued in his death. He was much beloved by all his fellow-labourers for his kindly and obliging disposition, securing the love of friends by the outgoing of his own love to them. Not only was he most dilligent and skillful in his department of duty, but he was ready for every good work, taking part of the burden of conducting the affairs of the congregation, with all willingness. Mr. Paton, who had been a worker like Mr. Bishop, in the evangelistic efforts in Edinburgh, has entered as his successor in his important department of Mission work.

In looking back on our records of by-past times in order to draw up the memoir, I felt that King Èyö VII. was highly worthy of being known, and his name held in remembrance among his countrymen. Our own countrymen will moreover, see in him a proof of the power of the Gospel, in raising an African king out of heathenism, and in sustaining him through a long life in his Christian profession, in the discharge of public duties as in private matters. He devotedly accepted and discharged the work of promoting the cause which Christ has committed to all His followers.

In this tractate I have gone over part of the ground over which I formerly travelled in "Calabar and its Mission." For this I offer no apology, as my subject required it.

H. G.

To those who may be curious to know the correct pronunciation of the Efik words occurring in the narrative, the following note will suffice as a guide.

The alphabet consists of twenty letters, or including the marked vowels and nasal ñ, of twenty six. Each letter has its one uniform sound. The vowel powers are thus noted—

A,   as in *fat, father*.
Ā,   as in *all, what*.
E,   as in *men, met*.
Ē,   as in *there*, and *a* as in *fate*.
I,   as in *racine, marine*.
Ī,   as in *bid, did*.
O   as in *so, note*.
Ŏ,   as in *nor, not*.
U,   as in *bull, full*.

CONTENTS.

———•———

MEMOIR OF KING ËYÖ HONESTY VII.

CHAPTER I.

THE COUNTRY.

On the west coast of Africa, sixty miles to the north-east of the island of Fernando Po, the Cross River pours its flood into the Gulf of Guinea. At the distance of forty miles from its mouth, the river divides into two main branches. On the one to the right in ascent, lies Duke Town, off which in bypast times lay the ships of the white man receiving the export of the country, and where the factories are now built. In the estuary between these branches, numerous islets divide the waters, connected by winding creeks, as they are called, on one of which lies Creek Town, which with Duke Town shares the principal part of the traffic of the country. Sailing among these islets, each reach of the river closed in by its windings, gives the pleasurable feeling of passing through

B

a succession of lakes, surrounded by the luxuriance of the
vegetable world.

The people of Efik, the country known to the world
as Old Calabar, were according to tradition driven out of
their native seat, Ibibio, by the conquerors in a tribal
war, and scattered themselves along the estuary of the
river, into the various settlements in which we now find
them.   The refugees in their descent found slave-ships in
the river, engaged in what was then the sole traffic of the
country, which was carried on till within two years of the
entrance of the United Presbyterian Mission, when it was
abandoned on the chiefs entering into a treaty with Britain.
The Calabar, which has mistakenly got the name of the
Cross River, was a principal seat of the slave-trade, so
that the region of the continent to which the river gives
entrance was very much despoiled of its population.   The
Calabar people were employed in hunting the neighbouring tribes, or acting as middle men in selling the captives
of the slave-raiders in the interior.   To capture or avoid
capture was the chief aim of the life of the people.   Under
its influence they were reduced very much to the condition
of the wild inhabitants of their forests, and out of this
there evolved customs of terrible atrocity.   British ships
had for several hundred years been frequenting the river,
but the only effort our countrymen ventured to make in
rebuke of the profuse slaughter of human victims, was to

stipulate that the murders should not be perpetrated in sight of the shipping.

But the slave-raid still continues. The tribes of the dark continent seem to be considered by superior races as made to be enslaved or destroyed, and the "open sore of humanity" which Livingstone lamented, is yet unhealed. Not only so, but the efforts in which he laid down his life in opening a way for the entrance of the Gospel, the only healing power, into the continent, at the same time opened a channel through which a flood of firewater pours in on every side. The European powers which have divided the territory of the dark-skinned tribes amongst themselves, by entering into engagements to protect them so far from these means of destruction, have given a hope that they will use their power to promote the gracious purpose of our common Father, that the Negro shall have his equal place among his fellowmen. But the hope is yet distant of accomplishment. When shall the commerce of the nations become "Holiness to the Lord?"

The refugees from Ibibio seem to have located themselves as they had been divided in their native villages, in various districts, named Mbiabo, Adiabo, Öbutöñ, and Iboku, which last includes Duke Town and Creek Town. The people of Öbutöñ (Old Town) were, at the first location, nearest the shipping, and taking advantage of their position, endeavoured to secure the monopoly of the trade. To prevent this, a number of the Creek Town families threw themselves farther down the river than Old Town, and procuring land from the Quä (Aba-kpa) tribe, built New Town, now called Duke Town (Atakpa).

The state of society, now changing, is patriarchal. The power of the head of a family is in this system absolute, in all things civil and sacred. He officiates as priest, presenting the worship of the household to *Ekpo*, the spirit of their ancestors. The people of the Iboku district, and apparently the whole of the tribe, had formerly also a tutelary deity, called *Ndem Efïk*, which was under the care of a priest entitled *Äböñ Efïk* (chief of Calabar), who doubtless once held the power with the title. His office, however, put such restrictions upon him as quite prevented him from engaging in foreign traffic, by which their wealth is chiefly made, so that for a long time the office has not been sought after.

The entrance of the Gospel into this state of pagan-ism very speedily made itself felt in the whole com-munity, and this, not only amongst those who gave ear to its teaching, but also in the condition of those who remained ignorant of it. Most of such then, and many now, refuse to acquaint themselves with the message of Divine truth and mercy, though enjoying its benefit,

allowing that the doctrine we preach and the mode of
life it enjoins may be all very right and good for us,
but they have their own modes of thought, and their
own way of life, which they prefer. So in regard to
our whole race of mankind. "The dayspring from
on high" came unthought of, unsought for, and was even
in most cases, rejected. So it still fares in seeking
an entrance into any tribe. King Ëyö II. in in-
terpreting the address of the missionary to the audience
met in his yard on Sabbath morning, most of them
being his own slaves, frequently said to them, that
those in their condition should be ready of all men to
give ear to the Gospel, for the Word of God had greatly
improved their condition. He could not do towards
them now as he had done formerly. It had much enlarged their liberty, though serfdom still remained.
Even in Christian communities enjoying the high civilization which the Gospel brings in its train, there will be
seen those who, enjoying that blessing, decry its source.
Walking in open day, and enjoying its splendour, they
bravely cry out, "We have abundant light without the
sun ! Away with it !"

By the gradual abolition of those atrocious customs
of barbarism to which I have referred, the whole tribe
has been raised from its former degradation. Life
and its comforts, scanty as these latter may be, are now

much more safely possessed. A considerable number abandoning their former heathen superstitions and rites, have been gathered into the churches planted by the Mission, and these, united to Christ as His people, claim kindred to all of every race who form His family.

As will be stated in order, the coast of the Niger region has been assumed as a protectorate by Britain. The first Consul-General of this territory, Major Sir Claude M. MacDonald, K.C.M.G., now holding the office, is one highly qualified for administering the power committed to him over the various tribes under his care. He is fully in sympathy with them, and anxious to aid them in every step which can be taken for their advancement.

CHAPTER II.

KING ËYÖ HONESTY II.

KING ËYÖ II., surnamed " Honesty," was in power when the Mission entered.   He got this addition to his official title from the European traders on account of his trust-worthiness in fulfilling his engagements with them.   He was one of six brothers, who each in succession inherited the title.

Ëyö II., when he came into the headship, rebuilt the town, which had been scattered by the contentions of his predecessor, the father of this memoir.   According to report, he went out into the public street, and lifting a handful of sand, he scattered it, proclaiming that thus he cast all strifes to the wind, and called upon all who had retired to the country districts to return and rebuild. He was a man of singular prudence and industry. In his boyhood he had been with Duke Ëfium, who has

given his name to Duke Town, and received from him
the wise advice, followed out by the Duke himself,
"Keep to your trade, and your trade will keep you."
This maxim King Éyö took as the rule of his life, and it
made him a man of peace, of wealth, and of power. He
was always very anxious to prevent, or to bring to a settlement, the strife which so frequently arises between
neighbouring tribes in the country, and submitted much
to injuries from them for the sake of peace.

However, when he could take redress of wrong in a
quiet way he was not slack to do so. A woman, one of
his slaves, threatened that if he did not give her more
kindly treatment she would run off to the Äkäyön tribe.
Quite a number of his people were fugitives in Äkäyön,
and on this threat he resolved to put an end to this
practice. He instructed his people who occupied farms
on the border of Äkäyön to make a midnight raid into it,
and carry off two or three of the principal men of the
tribe. This was done, and the captives were set free
when Äkäyön delivered up his people who had been
received by that tribe. The poor people did not better
their condition by their flight : being strangers, they
rather fared worse. More recently six fugitives, slaves
from Duke Town farms, made their escape in a canoe
to Äkäyön. All were murdered except the one woman
of their number.

His industry was also conspicuous. His books were always beside him, in which he noted in full detail the transactions of his people doing business for him in the various markets ; and when he had outdoor work in the town to attend to, he sat under a large umbrella on the side of the street, with his day-book before him on a table, attending to his market accounts while overseeing the work.

He was, moreover, very desirous of the advancement of his country. When the treaty, pressed upon the chiefs by Britain, to renounce the slave trade was agreed to by them, King Eyö addressed the following application to Commander Raymond, who negotiated the treaty :—

"Creek Town, December 1, 1842.

"To Commander Raymond, Man-of-War Ship *Spy*.

"I am very glad you come and settle treaty proper, and thank you for doing everything right for me yesterday. Long time I look for some Man-of-war, and when French man come I think he want war, and send one canoe to let you know, but too much wind live for him catch Fernando Po, and no one come help me keep treaty as Mr. Blount promise, and when I no give slaves French Man-of-war come make plenty palaver, but I no will. One thing I want for beg your Queen, I have too much man now, I can't sell slaves, and don't know what for do for them. But if I can get some cotton and coffee to grow, and man for teach me, and make sugar cane for we country come up proper and sell for trade side I very glad. Mr Blyth* tell me England glad for send man to teach book and make we understand God all same

* A trader in the river.

C

white man do.   If Queen do so I glad too much, and we must try do
good for England always.   What I want for dollar side is proper India
Romall and copper rods, I no want fool thing, I want thing for trade
side, and must try do good for Queen Victoria and all English woman.
I hope Queen and young King can live long time proper, and I am,
Sir, your friend."

(Signed)   "KING ÉYÖ HONESTY."

The instruction in agriculture which was thus
solicited, was contemplated on laying the scheme for
the Mission, but it was laid aside, our means enabling
us only to attend to our chief purpose, the introduction
of the Gospel.   Now, however, the work has been taken
up.   The Rev. William Risk Thomson of the Jamaica
Mission has resigned his charge of Lucea congregation,
and has been appointed by the Mission Board to
superintend the establishment of an Industrial Institu-
tion similar to that of Lovedale.   The Consul-General
has given a site in the neighbourhood of Duke Town,
and Mr. Thomson has commenced operations.

Éyö condemned the barbarous customs of the tribe,
and seeing that knowledge gave the white man his
superiority, he cordially used his influence to promote
the work of the Mission in education and civilization.
He collected a large audience in his public yard
every Sabbath for the missionary to address, and acted
as interpreter so long as his assistance in this way was
needed.   He sometimes offered objection to the doctrine

of the preacher, but he did not fail to speak out what was taught, and afterwards discussed it with his fellow-chiefs. When, however, the discourse met his views, he frequently enlarged on what the missionary uttered, and could speak to the people with more effect than he. When this help was no longer needed, a small church having been built, the King continued to attend the service regularly, and exhorted others to do so.

The native custom was to observe an eighth day Sabbath, though marked with little difference of observance from other days, but when the King was informed of the Divine institute of the seventh day Sabbath, he regularly observed it. Shortly before his death, when at a distance making a clearance in the forest to prepare for cultivation, he abstained from his labour on Sabbath and called on one of his slaves, a member of the church, to read and expound a portion of Scripture to him and his assembled labourers. He was a man before his time. He had thrown away the objects of heathen worship before the Mission came; and from the time of the entrance of the Gospel "He did many things," and "heard gladly."

CHAPTER III.

ËYÖ VII. IN HIS YOUTH.

KING Ëyö VII., Ensa Äkähä by name, better known formerly among our countrymen as Henshaw Tom Foster, was a young lad when the Mission entered. It was the custom in those days for the chiefs to place their boys on board the ships which lay in the river awaiting their cargoes, that they might pick up a little English and a knowledge of the traffic. Any skill in reading was then gained from the notes and entries of transactions in the books of the traders, so that it was the language as written which they could read. This induced the Rev. Mr. Waddell, the pioneer of the mission, to lithograph in this style the first simple lessons he printed for the instruction of the natives. The name of the captains with whom the boys were placed was frequently assumed by them. Hence the name Tom Foster.

Mr. Waddell, after twenty-eight years of energetic and successful service in Jamaica and Calabar, retired from the field in impaired health in 1858 ; but on regaining strength he devoted himself to the work of the church at home, in which he has been enabled to take a part, until approaching ninety years of age, though now the infirmities of age close his day of labour, and he waits for his call home.   His wife, as devoted to the work of the mission, lately entered into rest.   A long life of united service was granted them, and their works remain to bless succeeding generations.   In giving to the Mission Committee a statement of the condition of the church at Creek Town when about to take his departure, he says :

"In my last annual report I stated that I hoped soon to receive several more of the catechumen class to baptism ; but as the time draws near for quitting the country, I thought it best to leave that work to Mr. Goldie, as he would have the pastoral oversight of them when I would be gone.   One of those most anxious to be baptised, was a fine young man, Ensa Äkähä, of high country family, of mild and pleasing manners, and more than ordinary good conduct, for whose soul I have watched these many years past.   He had been at school in Mr. Jameson's time and subsequently, and was attentive in learning the Word of God.   For a long time afterwards, trading and farming took him away so much that I saw little of him. Whenever I met him, however, and admonished him about the truths of salvation, his duty to God and his own soul, he heard very seriously. During last year he came in our way more frequently, and seemed to be under spiritual concern. Young Ëyö, who succeeded his father as Ëyö III., interested himself for his spiritual welfare, being his cousin, and often brought him to church and class meetings. At the beginning of this year (1858) he came and declared himself, that he had fully made up his mind to serve the Lord. All last year, he said, he would have come forward, but that he wanted to bring his wife with him. She would not consent, however, to leave the customs and idols of her country and people, and at last left him to follow God's way himself."

Being thus free, he made no more delay in making public profession of his faith, and four months after Mr. Waddell's departure I had the great pleasure of admitting him into the church. Dr. Robb, who had recently transferred his services from the Jamaica to the Calabar Mission, and was at Creek Town at the time, thus speaks of him :—

" Having had a good deal of intercourse with Ensa, I have seen many gratifying things in his character. He seems to be quite emancipated from the superstitions of his people, and his one great desire is to know and follow the will of God in everything. It will be a blessed thing for Calabar and its neighbours, did all our young men manifest the same principle and the same seriousness as characterises Ensa."

Ensa was of a modest, retiring disposition, so that it was only the call of duty or the importunity of friends, which brought him forward to take his part in the town or in the church.

On the death of King Ëyö II., and of his son Ëyö III., though two of the family succeeded to the title, the slaves of the Ëyö clan adopted Ëyö Okün, one of themselves, as their head. He was the close companion of Ëyö III., and followed him in his policy as a peacemaker, and in opposition to customs of barbarism.

At that time King Asibön II. of Duke Town committed an atrocious act of cruelty, in laying waste a village of the Adiabo district of Calabar. A young man of the village had been shot accidentally, and his mother demanded the life of his unfortunate companion by whose hand he had fallen. Asibön, before whom she brought her demand, did not grant it, on which the woman, resolved in having blood for blood, hired some one to shoot the man slayer, but not finding him, he shot his brother. This satisfied the vengeful woman, but when Asibön heard that his verdict had been disregarded, he was furious, and demanded that the woman should be given up. The villagers very likely would not venture to put hands on a woman of her position, and on his requisition not being complied with, he summoned the whole of Iboku to vindicate his authority. The village was pillaged and burned, and all, young and old, who fell into the hands of the destroyer, were slaughtered, with the exception of those prisoners who were taken to Duke Town, to be killed at leisure. When Mr. Anderson, then in charge of Duke Town Station, heard of this, he went to Asibön and endeavoured to procure the release of the prisoners. He furiously answered that he would kill man, woman, and child, and if any had found refuge in a neighbouring tribe, he would demand them, and if not given up, he would make war on the tribe protecting them. Mr. Anderson, finding that Asibön would not listen to him, applied for help to the white traders in the river, who on hearing the case went to Asibön, and so vehemently denounced his attrocities, that he yielded, on condition that the prisoners should be sent to Fernando Po. Èyö Okün sent a contingent to make the attack for the purpose of making as many prisoners as possible to save from slaughter. On its return, one young woman was brought to Creek Town as prisoner, on which Èyö rebuked his warriors, no more of the people having been brought in, saying, "I sent you to preserve life, not to kill." Asibön sent a messenger with the demand that the

young woman be given up to him : Eÿö resented this,
and Mr. Edgerley, then in charge of Creek Town Station,
hearing of the case, went and took her to the mission
house for security. "The King (Ëÿö V.)" Mr. Edgerley
writes, " called me and told me to give up the woman to
him, and he would protect her, I replied that she was safe
where she was. A few more messages passed between his
majesty and me, and the matter dropped. In the evening
I saw Ensa Tom Foster, who knew what I had done, and
he promised to advise the king what to do. Early in the
morning I went to the king's yard ; request was again
made for the woman and again declined. The king seemed
rather pleased that I had got the woman. The turn affairs
had taken saved him from giving offence either to the
church party, by delivering her to death, or to the other
party, in refusing to give her up. We talked for some
two hours. Two of the chiefs spoke, opposing the King's
demand. Ensa told them what they should do to please
God. I was glad to hear one who had a seat in the council of the town quoting the Word of God, and urging
their duty on his fellow chiefs. One other was there
who was once with us but is not now, who also told the
king and the others what God required of them. At last
the king signed a pledge that the woman would not be
hurt, but would be protected, and that if I would bring
her to him he would return her at once to stay till all

D

the disturbance was at an end.   Three of the chiefs, Éyö
Okün, Ensa Tom Foster, and Young Tom Éyö, appended
their names.   When Utïbe, the poor woman appeared,
the king spoke very kindly to her and told her not to
fear, but go to the mission house until her heart became
brave."

Some time after this an incident occurred which test-
ed Ensa's sincerity and steadfastness in his profession.
The people of Duke and Creek Towns at this time mono-
polised the foreign trade, barring access to the ships to
the tribes farther up the river, and to their own countrymen in the surrounding villages.   One day a canoe came
down the river with its cargo of palm oil, and those in
charge requested the Rev. W. C. Thomson, then at
Ikünëtü, to put one of his Calabar lads on board, that
under his guidance they might break through the barrier.
Mr. Thomson was wishful to make the attempt, and put
a lad on board who had been placed in his household by
Ensa.   King Asiböñ got to know this, and he with the
other native traders of Duke Town, improved the opportunity thus offered to persecute Ensa.   They well knew
that he had nothing to do in the matter, but they demanded that he should take an oath by mbiam to this
effect, or pay a fine of between two and three hundred
pounds.   Ensa withstood the temptation, refused to
commit an act of idolatry, and met their exorbitant

demand, though it crippled him in his business for a long time.

In 1867 war broke out between Calabar and Äkäyöñ. This teritory lies between the two main branches of the river, immediately behind the farm districts of Creek Town and Ikünëtü, and is possessed by a small tribe, probably an emigration from Ädädöp, beyond the great Quā river. The inhabitants rejoice in their wild freedom, and this feeling, with their distrust of each other separates them, so that each family has its own settlement in the bush, living a life of thorough independence, nor have they yet so far modified this, as to form the community of a town. Their mutual distrust and their dread of the power of spells are so great, that they arm themselves when they go out of their own settlement, and formerly when sitting down to partake of food, they had the musket or matchet ready at hand. This cloud of dread overhangs the whole of their life, and takes all enjoyment out of it, leading them to seek occasional escape from it in wild drunken revelry. Into this wild tribe Miss Slessor, one of our Mission agents, entered four years ago. She was cordially received, and is treated with all respect, as she visits their various farm hamlets with the Divine word of light and love, healing the sick, rescuing those whom their superstition dooms to death, expending her kindness on them in every way, and thus giving herself to a

labour which few would undertake. She is making an
impression upon them, denouncing vehemently their customs of blood, and teaching more confidence in each
other, herself being the connecting link.

A feud, never quite forgotten, lies betwen Äkäyöñ
and Calabar, which breaks out occasionally in warfare, as
happened at the above date. A quarrel arose at a
market near Ikünëtü in which three Äkäyöñ people
were killed. There was no attempt made to obtain
redress in a peaceful way, but the farm districts of Creek
Town and Ikünëtü were invaded, the houses plundered
and burned, and the people slaughtered, so that the
whole of Calabar was involved in the strife. It was
said that the chiefs at Duke Town resolved that the war
thus begun should be continued till Äkäyöñ was subdued,
and so an end put to the disquiet to which they were
continually exposed from that tribe. The people of
Äkäyöñ had no doubt their grievances also, and they
united to repel the attack from Calabar which they had
thus provoked. In their mode of bush fighting they could
repel in their forest any invasion from Calabar, and the
war which was carried on for several weeks did not result
in their subjection, if this was aimed at. Both tribes got
tired of it. Äkäyöñ could obtain only through Calabar
the articles imported by the ships such as salt, &c., and
made overtures which were agreed to. Both tribes found

themselves at the conclusion of the war much in the
position they were in at the beginning, after laying waste
the property of each other, and their mutual slaughter
giving them a number of heads to display as trophies of
their valour. In order that the peace-making might
stand good, Äkäyön insisted that a man should be
brought and buried alive, his spirit being invoked to
inflict all due penalties on the party violating the
treaty. This was of course refused by Creek Town,
and Duke Town withdrew, being out of the way of
harm from Äkäyön, so leaving Creek Town to settle
matters as best it could.

Every man amongst these tribes is a soldier, and
turns out armed when called to the field. At the sum-
mons of their chiefs the members of the church turned
out with the others. One Sabbath when an assault of
the enemy was resolved upon they refused to take the
field on that day, while those who had no reverence for
the sanctity of the day, made the proposed attack,
encouraged by a charm made by a juju man to secure to
them victory. They were repulsed with the loss of a
small cannon. Ensa, who had no liking for the war or
the purposes aimed at, hearing that an assault of the
strongest Äkäyön position was agreed on, went out with
his followers, but when he came to the rendezvous he
found that the leaders resolved to observe the usual

heathenish rites to obtain success. He was the only
member of the Church who could speak to them as an
equal, and he remonstrated with them. They replied
that it was their old custom they were observing. Ensa
replied that that was true. "They did so when they
knew no better, but now God would not wink at such
things." So he declined to join them, and addressing the
warriors who were busy preparing for the field by smear-
ing their bodies with war medicine to make themselves
invulnerable, he endeavoured to convince them of their
folly, but they made light of his warning, saying they
would try. He asked them why the medicine man did not
go to the fight seeing his charm was to give protection.
They said he was to stay in the camp to keep on making
his spells. Ensa withdrew, and they went forth to the
attack, in a short time returning in hot flight, broken and
discomfited.

A note from Asuquä Ekanem, our native agent at
Ikünëtü, where the troops from Duke Town mustered,
states—"The Duke Town people full here. Some of
them came to church yesterday and to school. They
went to cut down the bush on Saturday, resting on the
Sabbath, and they will go to war on Wednesday.
There is a great famine in the place, because the Duke
Town people eat up all the food and all the fowls they
can catch. They eat up every thing, and so some of the

mourning women, shut up lamenting the death of their husbands, wish to come here (the mission house) for refuge." Thus the poor people of Ikŭnëtŭ suffered as much from their friends as from their enemies.

Äkäyöñ threatened to burn Creek Town, and Ensa with his contingent returned to protect the town. . When the male population is in the field, the women coming out of their seclusion, take possesion of it, and they fall upon any man lounging about therein, and give him a sound beating. Ensa seems to have prevailed over the tumult-uous revelry of the inmates of the harems, who were making the most of their freedom, by threatening to give up the protection of the town, if they continued their tumult.

Äkäyöñ surrendered at discretion to Duke Town in the usual way, a messenger with *mfañ*, a fruit of a species of *Amomum* hanging from his neck, indicating that they were reduced to live on such wild fruit. The Duke Town troops, whose help in the war was given only in the cutting of bush, immediately withdrew, and left Creek Town and the others to bear the brunt of the contest. This was carried on a few days longer, and the messenger with *mfañ* was sent to those who were still in the field. Odŭt, a small tribe in the neighbourhood, was entrusted with the drawing up of the treaty of peace.

CHAPTER IV.

EYÖ VII. ELECTED KING.

KING ÉYÖ II. died in 1858, and his son and three of his brothers followed him in quick succession, leaving no member of the family to step into the throne. Ensa meanwhile kept himself in the back ground, taking no steps to obtain honour or influence, but in 1874 the town called him to the headship. The Rev. S. H. Edgerley thus writes, " After a year of something like anarchy, we have now a Christian King. Ensa has been elected by Creek Town and its dependencies. He was crowned in the church, and takes the title of King Éyö Honesty VII. He is a nephew of Éyö II. At the death of Éyö VI., the people looked to Ensa, but three chiefs, who had no right to the throne, resolved that Ensa should not be King on any account, ' lest he sell the country to God's white men.'" This triumvirate took possession of the insignia of royalty and Egbo, and ruled all. " Ensa took

the matter very quietly, acting on the advice given by a
friend, ' Do not trouble yourself.   If God wishes you to
be King, He will clear the way for you.'   Not long after
two of the chiefs were laid in the grave, and the third
showed himself so incapable that the people put him
aside, and insisted on Ensa becoming King.

   " An incident happened at this time which greatly
favoured him.   A dispute arose between Henshaw Town
on one side, and Duke and Creek Towns on the other.
Some difficulty was found in selecting a judge.   At last
Ensa was chosen, and his conduct in the matter gained
him great praise, and won him many friends.

   " When invited to take office, he laid two conditions
before the chiefs ;—First, that the King govern, and the
people submit to be governed according to the will of
God, so far as made known in the Bible, and that there
be no religious intolerance.—Second, that he be not the
King of a party, but that all the towns under him submit
to him undividedly.   These conditions after being discussed were accepted, written in English and Efïk, and
signed by King and chiefs, and in public assembly
he was crowned.   The ceremony took place in the
church, and the British Consul had the honour of
crowning him.   Prayer was then offered for King and
people, and the King addressed his subjects.   He invited
them to aid him in doing good, asked the same of the
E

Consul, and lastly addressed the agents of the mission, expressing the hope that God's blessing would continue on it, and urging that each member of it cease not day nor night to win sinners to Christ."

The King had been in the membership of the Church for several years, and held office in it. Aware that the heathen party was strong, and clung to the old custom of settling the cases coming before them in judgment by it, he addressed them in the above manner, by which he shewed that he would not violate his profession as a Christian, and only on the terms proposed could he accept of the headship." Mr. Edgerley very justly says of him, "In manner he is very quiet, but not the less observant. He would never rush at an object, but having begun to move towards it, he would not be easily turned aside. He and his wife are fellow-travellers Zionward. Both give help in the Sabbath School, and when not teaching sit down as scholars."

In consenting to take the headship of the town, he was aware that he undertook no easy task, and the trouble which he anticipated soon sprang up. Notwithstanding the pledge they had made to unite under him, a part of the town, called Mbaraköm, broke off.* Consul Hartly came up the river at the time, and the King

* Creek Town consists of three parts, each leading family of the town having its own division. This separation of families and their locations in towns is a hindrance to the work of the Mission.

informed him, that on this account he was unable to discharge the duties of his office, for which he was held responsible.   Having settled some causes brought before him in Duke Town, the Consul came to Creek Town and endeavoured to get the people of Mbaraköm to be faithful to their engagement.   Their headman alleged that they had signed the document at the King's coronation as witnesses.   The Consul would not listen to this, but he did not succeed in healing the division, which proved a source of constant disquiet and eventually of rupture.

On the death of King Asibön I. of Duke Town, large numbers of the serfs gathered from their country districts and took possession of the town.   They bound themselves by a blood oath to stand by each other and not permit the old custom, by which they especially suffered, of human sacrifice for the dead.   In administering this oath, a small wound was made in the arm and the drop or two of blood which flowed was tasted by the entrant to the league, and all evil imprecated on him, should he violate the pledge.   The law had been previously passed which abolished the by-past custom, but they were doubtful whether it would be kept, and so they made a display of their power, before which the chiefs were helpless. On the death of King Ëyö II. a large number of his people entered into a league in this manner, thinking that for so great a man, the laws might be set aside.

The blood people, as they were called, who were connected with Creek Town, feeling their strength, ere long
quietly put aside King Ëyö and chiefs; a force of them
entered the town and called before them certain parties
whom they accused of the death of members of the league.
They held their assize at the bush market, their camping
ground, at the entrance to the town, and executed three
persons.   The King hearing that they were raising a
charge against him of causing the death of Ëyö Okün
whom they had recognized as their head, went on board
a ship in the river.   At a meeting at Eseku, a farm
district, Ësiën Ë. Ukpabio and other church members,
who could not take the blood oath, asked them what
they had to lay to the charge of the King.   They replied
that they brought no charge against him and they wished
him to return and sit as judge in charges they wished to
make against the children of Ëyö II.   They of the farm
districts and the town's people gave a mutual pledge not
to seek each other's hurt, and on the day following they
went with great display and brought back the King.
Continuing their assize, the blood people sent messengers
to the mission house, to call a woman before them who
had taken refuge therein.   I declined to recognise any
authority in the case except that of the King, saying I
would give her up only on the promise of the King to try
the case himself, and whatever the verdict might be, that

she should in the meantime be returned to me. This stipulation I made, hearing that the woman was accused of taking the life of her husband by charms. I suspect that she intended his death, and made use of the charms, believing, no doubt, that they would accomplish her purpose. Her life was spared on condition of sending her to Fernando Po.

King Ëyö, seeing that the settlement made when he yielded to the importunity of the people and accepted the headship was broken, and his measures for the benefit of the community opposed by a party, eventually contemplated forming a new settlement, to which all who wished to remain loyal to him might remove. Mbaraköm declined his authority, and the blood people, in the powerful Ëyö clan, administered their own affairs without reference to him. In following out this scheme he abandoned the town and got temporary residence on board ship. At a meeting of the male members of the congregation, called to consider whether we could do any thing to remedy the state of matters in the town, it was agreed to send a deputation to the King to express sympathy with him and solicit his return. He received the deputation kindly, in a house given him and his household in Cobham Town, a suburb of Duke Town, but expressed no change of purpose. Joined by a number not connected with the Church, the members had a conference

with the children of Éyö II. and the leaders of the blood
people, and exacted terms of them to open up the way for
the return of their King. They also demanded of the
headman, whose party had plundered the farms of the
Mbaraköm people on their flight, that the spoil should be
brought back. This demand was refused, whereupon
those who had taken the business in hand put him in
chains. The fugitives had made public proclamation that
if their goods were not restored, they would send Egbo
to destroy the town, a threat which alarmed the town's-
people, who fled taking as many of their valuables with
them as they could carry, the greater part of them join-
ing the King.

With the terms they had secured the deputation
repeated their visit to the King, and put them before
him, who replied that he did not think they opened the
way for his return, but he would consult those who had
joined him, and give the result of their council. The
reply was, that he did not see his way to return, but ere
long he was prevailed upon to take this step and assume
his position. In the meantime, the deputation dis-
appointed in its object, appointed a committee of vigilance
to protect the town. This assumed authority was
acknowledged by all parties, and peace was secured.

CHAPTER V.

THE LATTER PERIOD OF HIS REIGN.

In the end of the year (1875) Mr. Edgerley returned from furlough, bringing with him a handsome Bible, the gift of a few ladies in Edinburgh to the King, in recognition of his efforts for the benefit of the people. Mr. Edgerley, in giving an account of his presentation of the gift, says,—" I asked the King to call his council next afternoon, thinking the opportunity too good to be lost, in presenting the gift of far off friends who had heard of the King, to show their admiration of his conduct. Around him were many supporters, but he had also powerful opponents in direct opposition to whom he had carried forward his past scheme of improvement, who were drags on the progress of the country. I knew that a public presentation would be encouraging to the King and his party, and discouraging to the opposition."

The council met, and in a suitable address Mr. Edgerley presented the gift. The following acknowledgement of the gift was made, and signed by all the members, all taking the gift as a friendly offering to the town:—" Ladies, we, the chiefs of Creek Town, rejoice much to see our friend Mr. Edgerley again, who tells us good words about the life of our souls in Jesus Christ, that by the grace of God, by hearing these words of life, through faith in Jesus we may possess this life.

" Our hearts rejoice very much on account of the book you gave to be presented to our King, which shows that you have good purposes and good thoughts concerning us. We beseech you not to forget us in the prayers you present to God, because we are still living in darkness. But we much are gratified that through the goodness of God, our King is a member of His Church, and knows to read His book and to explain it to us, as God enables him to do. We thank you very much. May you continue in comfort."

The Bible was the King's law book, and in endeavouring to enforce such of its enactments as could apply to our state of society, he had to fight against old customs. He prevailed upon the heads of the town to enact by proclamation, laws to provide for the better observance of the Sabbath in the town, and in country districts. It was thereby enacted, that no one, under a penalty, carry out a burden from the town on God's day, and no one bring a burden into the town; that no one go for wood or water, or fire a gun, or engage in any play; and that no canoe leave the beach, or come in, unless in a case of necessity.

Some time after he sent forth a proclamation, that all the children running about the street go to school, which at once more than doubled our number of scholars.

Every thing which concerned the Church was of the greatest interest to the King.   Our first place of worship becoming too strait for us, it was resolved to build one larger.   To encourage the native congregation, the Mission Board gave liberal aid, but as is the manner of the country, it was erected only after considerable delay. In his desire for its completion, the king in the name of the membership thus writes to the foreign Mission Com- mitee:—(23rd July 1878), " We need a new church very much.   When Mr. Edgerley was at home we been write to him to help us for the new church, and when he return, he and Mr. Goldie wish us to meet for school- house. Both members of the house of God, and the chiefs, and the people of the town, all meet together.   Then the Rev. H. Goldie and the Rev. S. M. Edgerley inform us concerning the new church, also show us the plan of it, which we are very glad to have. Some of us sign for so much rods they will give, and cut the posts ready to put

F

up the Church.   Mr. Edgerley told us that you kindly
promise to give £400 as a grant, and £400 as a loan to
the congregation, to be prepaid in yearly instalments, so
we think the erection may be begun during that dry
season, between November and March.   It was joyful
news to us all when we hear of this.   We beseech you to
help us according to your promise, that our joy not returned into sorrow.   We are very sorry about the eight
puncheons of palm oil in which the congregation's contri-
butions were sent to Liverpool, which was lost by steamer,
so we have not so much money for the church as we
looked to have at this time, but we will send the oil as
we promise.   We had expect the new church out on last
dry season but it did not come.   And we expect it here
on the beginning of this dry season, but we not heard any
thing about it, so we write this to remind you about it.
We hope it may come soon.   In name of the deacons,—
Ëyö VII."

The church prepared in Scotland came out in due
time.   It is a comfortable place of meeting, with a small
spire and public clock.   It accommodates between 500
and 600 comfortably, but between 700 and 800 are frequently crowded into it.   The day of its opening, July
5th, 1879, was made a great day by the King, who invited his friends from Cobham Town.   The congregation was reckoned about 1000 in number.

The opening of the church was further signalized by the ordination of Asuquö Ekanem as pastor of Ikünëtü.

Mrs. Edgerley thus narrates the event, "Saturday last was a day of great rejoicing here. Flags were flying, and guns were fired in the early morning by the King, to intimate to the people that it was a day of glad tidings, and at ten o'clock the new church bell rung out, calling all to the opening. The rain poured in torrents, notwithstanding the church was crowded, and many were obliged to go away. It was a pleasant sight to see. There were hearers from all the other towns, almost all dressed in European garments. Indeed the inclination at present is to err on the other side. Hats, feathers of every hue, flowers and veils. But this is an evil which will mend itself in time. The forenoon was devoted to the dedication and opening addresses, the afternoon to ordaining Asuquä Ëkanem to the pastorate of Ikünëtü. On Sabbath we held the communion. There were over ninety communicants belonging to this church, and also some from Ikünëtü, Ikröröfiöñ, and Duke Town, so that more than one hundred partook of the Lord's Supper. The chiefs of Ikünëtü sent down 600 rods, value £7 10s., as their offering, saying, they wanted to have a share in this thing.

Truly it is still the day of small things, but to those who remember the former days of darkness, and witness now the happy faces of these people, their joy over, and plea-

sure in, their new church, their determination that they
will yet pay back to the friends in the "white man's
country" the money so kindly lent them, one cannot
help saying "what hath God wrought?"

The credit of the successful completion of the building belongs to the late Mr. Edgerley, jun. I left on
furlough immediately after the opening, and in my
absence, the greater part of the loan was repaid, and he
induced the congregation to assume the gift also as a loan.
This has also been repaid, and thus the congregation has
met the whole cost of the building.

Some time after the king writes to Mr. Waddell
(26 July 1879), "I am glad in having the opportunity to
write you a few words. In the first place I thank God
for His everlasting goodness that we can still hear the
voice of each other yet in this life. We of Creek Town
are still having much interest in you as the one that had
been first sent to open the way for the rest to walk
thereby, with the same precious Gospel trumpet which is
still sounding.

"I can but say, that I am now feel very happy to see
that Calabar is not now entirely what it was in the
days of our fathers before your coming, and during the
time of your being among us. A great change has taken
place ever since, through the power of the Gospel, and
even until now, the evil customs are still gradually dying

away, and my desire and hope is, that the whole work of Satan may be destroyed in Old Calabar.   For it was true in part of Ëyö III.'s sayings, in recalling to mind what you said once to me by a letter, that it is a hard thing for a Christian man to be a king in Old Calabar ; but in the other way is not quite so true, for a real Christian should know first that he could not be able to do a single thing of his own power without the help of God. And thus I see that as long as a man of God keeps nearer and nearer to Him, he is able to make the heathen ones submit to him whether he is a king or is not.   However I am very much pleasing see in my day, that the civilization is now on the way of bringing down all the evil and wicked ways of Satan.   I hope this will find you and Mrs. Waddell quite well.   Mr. Goldie, who is coming home for a change, will tell you more about Calabar.   I trust that God will take good care of them in their going and coming.   I was very glad to see both Mr. and Mrs. Edgerley come back to do the work here among us ; and may God bless every one of them who are here to teach the people the way of truth.   May we all meet in Heaven to part no more from each other."

When the Mission entered the country, the chiefs in giving us settlements for our stations, stipulated that we would not go beyond Calabar.   Their fear was, that if if we went into the upper tribes where the oil markets are, our countrymen would follow, and buying at first hand, deprive native traders of their business as middle-men. In the meantime all our efforts being called forth in introducing the Gospel among a people whose language was unwritten, we accepted the stipulation. When we went to Ikörofiöñ, our first station at an oil market, though still in Calabar, a pledge was given that we should not take part in or interfere with the traffic. After a while we explored the region of the continent into which we had the prospect of extending the Mission. The more conservative of the chiefs would have hindered us, but King Ëyö stood our friend, saying, when their opposition was overcome, "God has unloosed the door, and wishes you to push it open." Mr. Edgerley, who took the lead in exploration at that time, thus writes to the Foreign Mission Secretary :—" I am glad to say that the old conservatism of the Umön people has begun at last to yield, and now after many fruitless attempts the people have allowed us to pass their town. The King gave his valuable help. He would have gone himself to Umön, but not being able to do so, he sent Prince Eyamba of Duke Town, our elder there, as an envoy, to assure the people that there is no danger, but there will be much good in receiving teachers and allowing them to pass to the upper tribes. The King had promised his help, so soon as I was in a position to use it, so on receipt of your note, it appeared to me time to push up the water-way of the Cross River. King Éyó, was better than his word, for as soon as he heard that I was preparing for a journey to Umön, he sent a messenger to let them know and assuring them of our good intention. So interested was he that he came down from his farm twenty miles up the river to consult with me and tell me what he had done.

I left Creek Town on Tuesday, and spent the night with the King at his farm. Prince Eyamba had arrived a few hours before. Among other things the King bade him remember, that he was going on God's work, and must not mix up any trade matter with it; and if Umön let me pass but stop him, he must wait in the Town till my return, a sort of hostage for my good behaviour. Next day the King conveyed us several miles and left us with many good wishes for our welfare and success. On our return I spent a night with him, when with a hearty laugh he said he could not get us out of his thoughts at all, and dreamed about us all night.

In course of time, when the people saw that we came as friends, the freedom of the whole continent was allowed us. Lately a formidable armed German force left Cameroons to explore the "hinterland," as they termed it. Going armed, the party met with opposition. Many of the natives fell before the arms of their invaders, who also suffered severely. The remnant of the company came out on the Binué in woful plight, and was succoured by the agents of the Niger Territory colony.   About that time two of our number in a small boat went up the Cross River and entered German territory.   The people seeing strangers turned out to guard their country, but when they found that the two strangers were defenceless and came as friends, they met with a friendly reception.

When the scramble among the European powers for possession of Africa began, Britain, which had not sought an addition of territory on the west coast, having been content with the stripe of seaboard so long occupied, was aroused to claim part in the division of the spoil.   In 1884 Consul Hewett came up the river, and invited the Calabar chiefs to accept of British protection.   The heads of Creek Town at once assented, while those of Duke Town hesitated, but joined with the others, on receiving the assurance that there was no intention of disturbing their social condition.   King Eyö informed me, that one reason which induced him to sign the treaty was, that the mission should not be injured by the entrance of the French, who however tolerant in Europe, in allowing equal scope to every form of Christian worship, are intolerant in their foreign possessions, and employ the Romish Church as a political power to advance their interest.   In 1891 the coast from Lagos to the Rio del Rey was consti- tuted " The Oil Rivers Protectorate," under Sir Claude

McDonald, who sympathises with, and takes a great interest in promoting the benefit of the tribes in his consulate.
King Ëyö's wish was that Calabar might be taken up as
a crown colony, but the existence of slavery prevents this
in the meanwhile, Sir Claude's purpose being gradually
to put an end to it. The power of those officials who
represent countries which have laid hold on Africa,
is in practice absolute, and should be entrusted only to
those who recognise the claims of justice on the part of
the natives, and who sympathize with them, so as to
employ their authority to lift them out of their barbarism.
The Gospel is the supreme power in this work of bene-
volence, but government has also its duty to discharge.

Anxious to promote the advancement of the mission,
the leading members of our congregations, a good many
years ago, formed a conference meeting at stated periods,
to consider how they could unitedly use their strength to
put down the barbarous customs still existing in the land.
In this conference it was resolved that a systematic
effort should be made towards self-support, and a finance
committee was elected which issued a paper indicating
the steps to be taken to this end. The plan was, to put
the money contributed in the various congregations into
a common fund, from which the native agents should be
supplied so far as the contribution allowed, the supple-
ment required, to be asked for from the Mission Board.

G

King Ëyö and Prince James Ëyamba in the name of the committee, drew up a circular pointing out these steps in order to educate the members of the congregations in the duty of each individual giving for the support of the church. It also recommends the practice of persons giving offerings to God out of their increase, in addition to the regular Sabbath collection. An unhappy rupture of the Duke Town church put an end to their wise schemes. Now the rupture has happily been repaired, the conference is revived, giving a hope that the scheme of self-support may be again taken up.

In 1891 the King thus writes to Mr. Anderson then in Scotland,—" My dearest friend, I am thankful to God that I am able to send you a few' words in writing. Although I have not the pleasure of seeing your face now, yet I am very happy the Lord has given us this great gift to read and write, so that we are able to send words to such a far country as England, and can get books from friends there, and read their writings as if we saw them face to face. On the 9th of April I took a trip to the country which is called Öfuöt Emüm ye Ita. The people there had heard about me, and came to one of my men who was there, with the message that I must send and open their new market for them, and also that they wished to be under my protection. I sent my people to open the market for them, and if the trade goes on, I shall send more people to live with them, and trade with them. On Thursday I took my first trip to pay a visit to them, and reached them the following day, because my canoe goes very quickly. On Saturday I sent to their headman who came to me on Sabbath. I had a meeting with them, and they all sat very quietly to hear what was spoken. On Monday, the chiefs from the interior came down to visit me. I had some conversation with them. They spoke of the good things of this life, and I took the opportunity of speaking to them about something far better,—the welfare of their souls for ever. Their way of living is just what you found in our country, Ëfïk, when you came here first. When we compare the present time with the time when the Gospel came, we see what great works of mercy the Lord has wrought among us. The chiefs in that part of the country were thirteen in number. I beg that you will kindly remember me to the Christian friends in your country, and I also ask your prayers that the Lord may spread His light to the dark parts of our land." Thus the King held it his duty to promote the kingdom of Christ as well as the temporal good of all around him.

As an instance how any claim of right by the weaker races is put aside by some of those who have appropriated the territory of the negro, professing to lift him into civilization, occurred after the British protectorate had been thrown over Calabar. On the 27th, of February 1889, the Consul, being absent at Bonny, a German gunboat from Cameroons came up the river. A native of Germany, who had for many years been a trader in Calabar. acted as guide to the officials so enabling them to carry out their purpose. He brought them up to a small factory at Creek Town, and sent an invitation to the King to meet with them. The King at once complied with the invitation, thinking that they wished to confer with him as to trade matters, but on his entrance into the factory he was made prisoner. Two men of that part of the town which had refused to acknowledge the King. had a trading station at Rumby, within the territory which Germany had appropriated. A quarrel arose between the Momoko people and those of Rumby, in which a woman belonging to the former was accidently shot. This enraged them, and in their fury they plundered Rumby village and burned it, carrying off six of the people belonging to the Creek Town men. In order to secure a return of their men, the Creek Town traders seized seven of the Rumby people and came off. The gunboat came to demand the delivery of the seven captives, bringing only one of the six people the Rumby natives had seized. King Ëyö knew nothing of all this, the two traders having gone to Ikünëtü, and made no report to him of what had occurred, but on the demand of the gunboat officers, he said that the men should be delivered as soon as possible.   Not satisfied with this assurance, they carried off the King and put him on board the gunboat lying off Duke Town, to be detained till the men appeared.   He took this outrage very quietly, and sent to ask Mr. Beedie for the loan of a Bible.   He sat quietly reading it on board, and the jests and scoffs of the officers passed by him unheeded.   The men demanded were brought on board on the following day and he was let go.   Returning the Bible to Mr. Beedie, he quietly remarked, "Our Father has delivered me out of the hands of these people."   The commander of the gunboat, to make something of his trip, after subjecting the King to this outrage, demanded a number of cows and goats, holding two of the headmen of the town as hostages till he got what he demanded.   The animals were got as soon as possible, but when carried down to the gunboat it was found that it had gone off with the two hostages. We heard that an apology was eventually made for this high handed procedure, but if so, no apology was made to King Ëyö.   Such transactions suggest the question, what civilization will our German neighbours introduce amongst the tribes over which they have taken the rule, when they could act thus even in a British protectorate?

Enyoñ is a small tribe located on the banks of the

Cross River above Calabar, and commanding the passage
of the upper part of the river, Umön being the farthest
place to which the Calabar canoes were formerly permit-
ted to go. Ndem Enö a chief of the tribe, taking
advantage of his position, had of late been plundering the
canoes, and sometimes capturing their crew. He acted
in concert with the people of Umön who barred the river
to all passage beyond them, so that all trade from or to
the up-river tribes might continue to pass through them.
The Consulate powers wished to make the river passage
free to all the tribes on its banks, and the Consul *pro tem.*
sought an interview with Ndem Enö. He was desirous
to put a stop to this piracy, without recourse to arms, but
Enö kept out of the way. The Consul then summoned
the Europeans in the factories and Calabar chiefs, to get
their aid in bringing Ndem Enö to terms, peacefully, if
possible. King Eyö and others advised the seizure of
Ndem Enö, as on the approach of war canoes, he would
get out of the way, and people innocent of his misdeeds
would be those who suffered ; but the young men, white
and black, declared for an attack. Preparation was
accordingly made, and while the King kept himself aloof,
some of the head men of Creek Town took part in it,
acting as they said, at the command of the Consul. Mr.
Johnstone, a young man carrying on mission work at
Umön on his own account, mediated between the parties

to bring the matter to a peaceful issue, but failed. Ndem Enö's people when the attack was made fired off their guns and then fled, while the Calabar forces plundered and burned the farms along the brink of the river. One or two of their number were wounded, and a few of the Enyoñ people were shot. What was clearly to be anticipated happened. Ndem Enö took himslf out of the way of harm, and when the fall of the river prevented the employment of a gunboat by the Consul, he returned to his old location and his former practice. This conduct of Ndem Enö, by which, in concert with the people of Umön, he endeavoured to maintain the blockade to protect their monopoly, for several months interrupted intercourse with the mission stations in the upper part of the river. They would not have barred the passage of a canoe or boat which they knew belonged to the mission, but the Calabar people in terror of the Enyoñ chief, refused to furnish a crew. Two of our number who were invalids had left their stations to find a passage to Britain, were detained, and in order to carry out their purpose they journeyed across the country to find a passage by the other branch of the river. They came out at Uwet, where they were hospitably entertained by Ĕfiüm Otu Eköñ, formerly one of our teachers, who has taken up his residence there, and has gained a considerable power in the district, which he employs for good, and acts as

an evangelist. When he heard that our friends were
shut up at Ikotana he sent a quantity of provisions
across the country, fearing they might be in need.

King Ëyö died on 26th of March 1892. To the end
of his life he maintained his character as a sincere
Christian, and was ever ready to take part in any scheme
to promote the welfare of the community. He acted
under the persuasion that "there is nothing in our life,
in which God is not interested, where He is to be absent.
There is nothing wherein we may not glorify and obey
Him."* The King received the instructions given us
in Scripture regarding the conduct of the various business of daily life, with the unquestioning obedience of the
child, and in the discharge of his official duties especially
this was manifest. In doing the world's work, in the
eager pursuit of it, many of those claiming the position
of Christians forget God, and employ all their capacity,
mental or physical, not to please Him, but to secure their
own aims, thus making the duties of the present life
hindrances not helps in the way heavenward, as they
should be. Even in politics which should be kept uncon-
taminated by unworthy principle or motive, self-seeking
often polutes them, and

     "Gives up to party what was meant for mankind."

It will amuse some, no doubt, that the King should

* Adolphe Saphir's *Hidden Life.*

go back to the time of Nehemia, and copy his legislation, but it would be well if those whose office is to govern nations or cities, if they did not transfer the laws of the Jewish legislator to their own measures, drew nearer to them. The King's proclamation for the observance of the Sabbath does not now command the obedience required, but the sacred day in Creek Town is as well observed as in any town in Scotland.

In his latter years he had frequent ailments, and at last sank under an attack of paralysis. As the disease gained upon him, he became unable to speak, but his long consistent life was testimony of his sincerity, beyond any other that could be given. During his reign he had to withstand opposition in the duty of his office from those wed to old superstitions and customs, and in his Christianity the scoffs and ridicule of those opposed to all change, and of many of our fellow countrymen. He was, notwithstanding, much respected by his people for his integrity and skill in counsel, so that he was frequently sought as a judge in important cases between parties. His influence extended far beyond Creek Town, especially in promotion of the work of the mission, in which he saw the regeneration of the country.

He entertained an ardent desire for the abolition of slavery, and he left his own people, except a few which he retained in personal service, to attend to their own

H

interests as they judged best.   He would have been highly
gratified, had Britain taken up the country as a crown
colony and so at once secured freedom to all.   The greater
part of the population, though nominally slaves, are prac-
tically free to follow their own business, but he longed to
see even the state of serfdom which prevailed abolished,
and as his ailments increased, he sometimes expressed
the sorrowful apprehension that he might not live to see
his desire accomplished.

King Ēyō, as has been stated, was modest and retiring,
and waited on invitation, even frequently requiring ur-
gency, to induce him to undertake any duty beyond
what belonged to his office.   The congregation elected
him to the eldership, in which he acted as clerk of session,
and for a while as superintendent of the Sabbath School.
Eventually he was persuaded to take charge of the first
meeting for public worship in the early morning of the
Sabbath, and when necessary, conducted the public worship of the pulpit in a very acceptable and efficient
manner.   He had an extensive and accurate acquaintance
of scripture truth, consulting his small library of English
authors, but he was very much a man of one book, and
that book was the Bible, in perusing which he spent much
time.   In any serious case involving life which came
before him as judge, he generally informed the missionary at the station, and was scrupulously anxious to

administer his rule, as he had pledged himself at his coronation, according to Divine law.

When the Rev. Messrs Marshal and Williamson as deputies from the Mission Board visited the Calabar Mission in 1881, King Ëyö was highly gratified by the kindness shown by the home Church in their visit, and paid them all attention in his power. In giving an account of their intercourse with him they thus write,—"We have a great regard for King Ëyö; during our stay we learned to esteem him very highly, and he laid us under obligations by many acts of considerate kindness. We hope, then and think also, that he will not consider us disrespectful or ungrateful if we venture to give a distinct conception of him to our readers. He is a big *soncy* man, perhaps forty years of age, with a pleasant countenance, of an unaffected dignity, quiet, sagacious, capable of shrewd remarks, and relishing a joke. But for his colour you would take him for a Scotchman. We asked him to come to the Synod, assuring him of a hearty reception and he jocosely asked in reply, whether in the event of his going we would take his place till he returned. He was much gratified by a deputation coming to his country, the first visit of the kind ever paid, and it was to put honour on the occasion that he met us so handsomely on our arrival, and conveyed us so comfortably to his town."

In his death I lost a sincere personal friend, as well as

a zealous and efficient worker in the congregation. He was ever ready to meet any claim on his kindness, and esteemed it a pleasure, even at much effort, or inconvenience to himself, to give any aid which he saw would be required. When Mrs. Goldie was attacked by a disease which threatened her life, he went down during the night to bring up the doctor, and when she died, he prepared her grave, over which the women of the congregation have raised a memorial stone.

He was raised up in the midst of the densest heathenism, showing what the Gospel by the grace of God can do, in lifting him above the pagan customs of his country, and enabling him to maintain a life becoming his Christian profession.

www.ingramcontent.com/pod-product-compliance
Lightning Source LLC
Chambersburg PA
CBHW022156020726
47496CB00008B/2737